A BULLETIN BOARD BOOK FOR ALL SEASONS

by

Susanne Glover
Georgeann Grewe
Mark Kuhns
Ronald Paugh
Deborah Prezioso
Illustrated by Georgeann Grewe

ISBN No. 0-916456-79-X

Printing No. 123456789

GOOD APPLE, INC.
BOX 299
CARTHAGE, IL 62321

TO THOSE WHO HAVE WORKED DILIGENTLY TO CREATE THESE BULLETIN BOARD IDEAS TO PROMOTE THE BETTERMENT OF STUDENTS AND TEACHERS AROUND THE WORLD.

AUTHORS: SUSANNE GLOVER
GEORGEANN GREWE
MARK KUHNS
RONALD PAUGH
DEBORAH PREZIOSO

ILLUSTRATOR: GEORGEANN GREWE

TYPIST: DEBORAH PREZIOSO

TABLE of CONTENTS

FLIP into FALL

WHIZ into WINTER

SPRINT into Spring

TEACHERS THROUGHOUT THE COUNTRY HAVE BEEN SPENDING MORE AND MORE TIME DEVELOPING A STIMULATING ENVIRONMENT FOR LEARNING. ONE OF THE BASIC NEEDS IN TODAY'S CLASSROOM IS IMPROVED PENMANSHIP. WE, THE AUTHORS OF THIS BOOK, HAVE DEVELOPED A PROGRAM TO IGNITE AND INSPIRE PRIDE IN STUDENTS' HANDWRITING. OUR PROGRAM CONSISTS OF BULLETIN BOARD IDEAS SUITABLE FOR HANDWRITING DISPLAY AND MAY BE ADAPTED TO OTHER CONTENT AREAS.

We gott'em for autumn, we gott'em for spring,
We gott'em for just about any old thing.
They're easy to make and pretty to see,
And will brighten your room so creatively.
With pictures, ideas and patterns galore,
Browse through the book to see what's in store.

TITLE: KICK-OFF TO A NEW YEAR

MATERIALS:

1. Yellow background
2. Two enlarged football players and footballs
3. Goal post made from brown paper
4. Brown construction paper for block letters to spell KICK OFF TO A NEW YEAR
5. Brown construction paper for footballs (pattern on next page)

USE IN CONTENT AREAS:

1. Reading: Use to introduce new stories or characters.
2. Spelling: Kick off a new spelling unit by listing new words on the footballs.

EXTENSION:

This bulletin board could be used in September at the beginning of the school year or in January to begin a new calendar year.

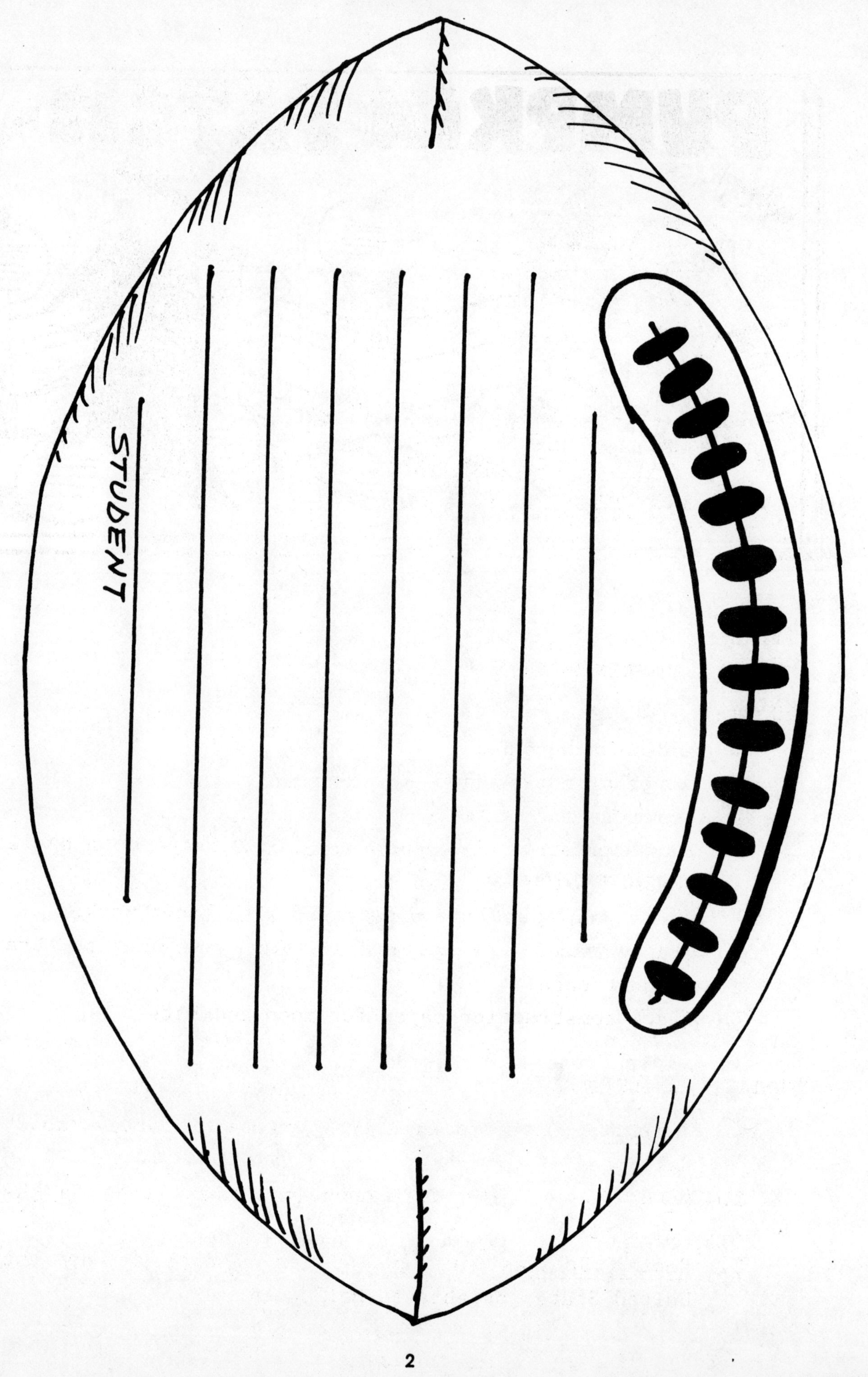
STUDENT

TITLE: PUMPKIN PATCH

MATERIALS:

1. Yellow background
2. Green construction paper for grass
3. Brown log-style fence
4. Brown construction paper for block letters to spell PUMPKIN-PATCH
5. Large yellow cornstalk outlined with brown marker
6. Orange pumpkins outlined in black marker (pattern on next page)
7. Black construction paper for moon and bats

USE IN CONTENT AREAS:

1. English: Develop creative writing stories about Halloween.
2. Math: Place individual problems of any type on the pumpkins.
3. Social Studies: Assign written reports on why the United States celebrates Halloween.

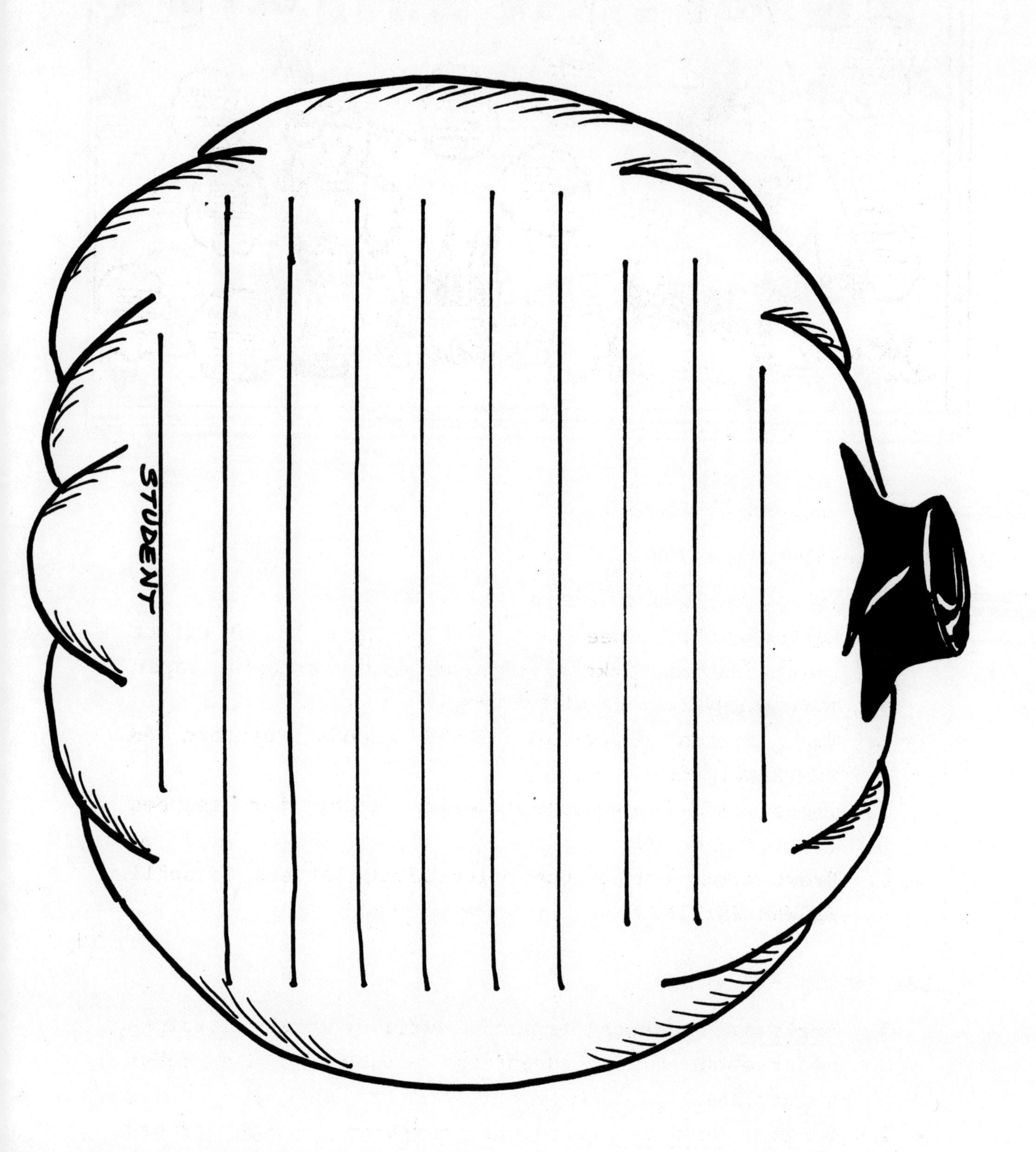
STUDENT

TITLE: WIGWAM WRITINGS

MATERIALS:

1. Yellow background paper
2. Large brown teepee displayed to give a 3-D effect
3. Indian making smoke signals-use brown wrapping paper and various colors of markers
4. Construction paper for smoke clouds (pattern on the next page)
5. Orange and brown construction paper for teepees (pattern included)
6. Brown construction paper for block letters to spell WIGWAM WRITINGS

USE IN CONTENT AREAS:

1. English: Students develop creative writing assignments about Indian adventures or create Indian rebus writings.
2. Social Studies: Students research Indian tribes and beliefs.

STUDENT

TITLE: BOARDING FOR (name of school)

MATERIALS:

1. Yellow background paper
2. Black construction paper for block letters to spell BOARDING FOR ____________________
3. Large picture of a school bus (back view) outlined with black
4. White construction paper for smoke puffs
5. Black construction paper rectangles cut slightly larger than the white boarding pass (pattern included)

USE IN CONTENT AREAS:

1. Math-Place individual problems of various types on passes with answers written under a "destination sign."
2. Beginning of school-Use as a source of information about your class.

BOARDING PASS

STOP

NAME: ____________________

ADDRESS: ____________________

PARENT: ____________________

DATE OF BIRTH: ____________________

SCHOOL: ____________________

BUS NO: __________ HOME PHONE: __________

__________ AGE

__________ TEACHER

TITLE: BLAST OFF....into the NEW YEAR!*

MATERIALS:

1. Medium blue background paper
2. A drawing of a rocket
3. Aluminum foil to cover parts of the rocket to give a shiny appearance
4. White construction paper for stars
5. Black construction paper for block letters to spell BLAST OFF INTO THE NEW YEAR

USE IN CONTENT AREAS:

1. Reading- Use to introduce new reading book. Label stars with chapter titles.
2. Social Studies-Use with a study of customs celebrating the coming of a new year.

*This could be used in September at the beginning of the school year or in January to begin the calendar year.

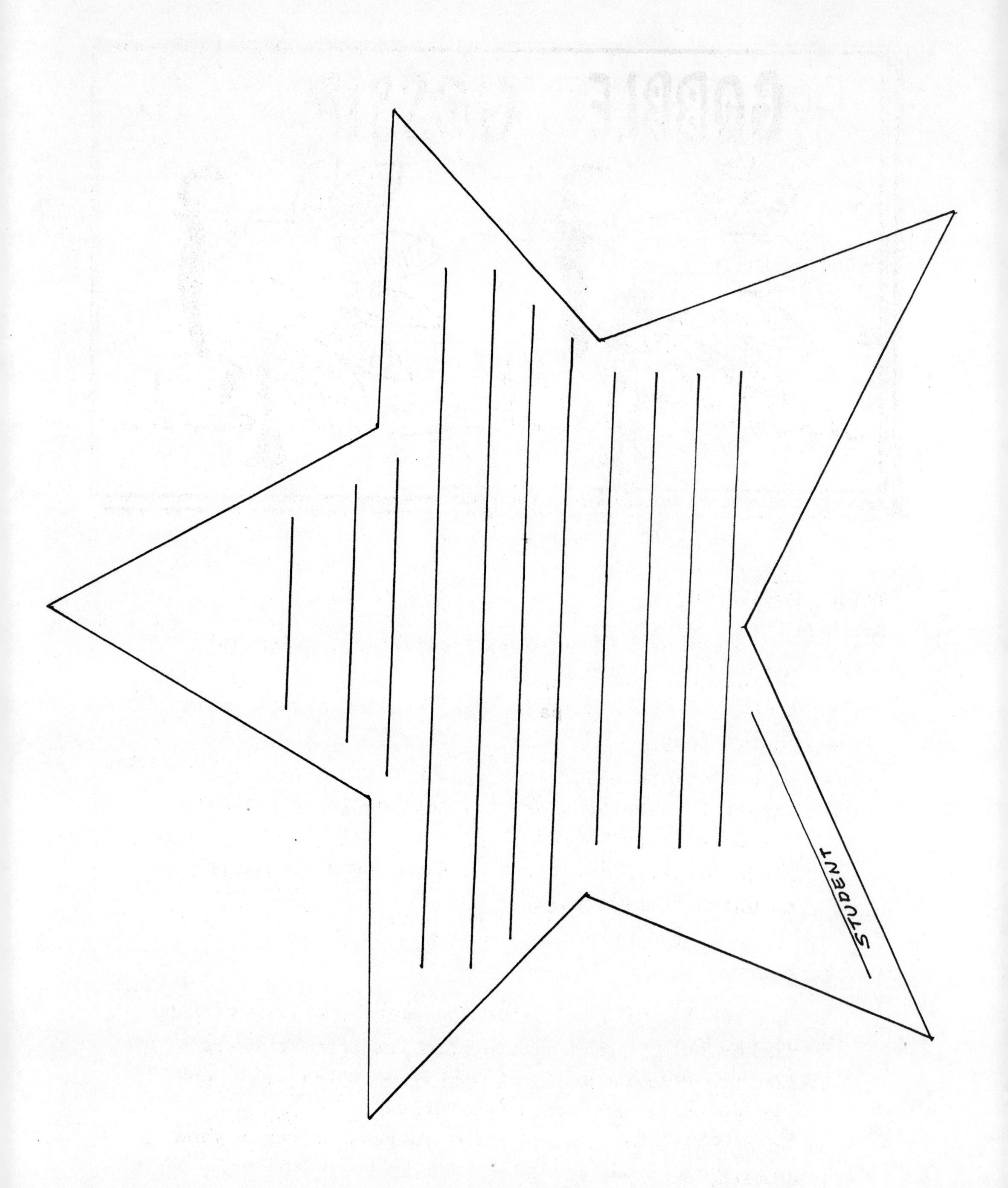
STUDENT

TITLE: GOBBLE GOSSIP

1. Two large brown turkey bodies (without feathers)
2. Yellow background paper
3. Brown construction paper for thin letters to spell GOBBLE GOSSIP
4. Brown construction paper feathers cut slightly larger than white paper feathers on which children write (pattern included)
5. Brown or green construction paper used as ground on which turkeys walk

USE IN CONTENT AREAS:

1. English-Assign tall tales that can be developed into turkey tales (Thanksgiving stories about turkeys).
2. English-After a study of quotation marks, dialogues can be written between two turkeys.
3. Science-Assign reports about turkeys or other game animals.
4. Creative writing-Assign reports about family customs or traditions of Thanksgiving.

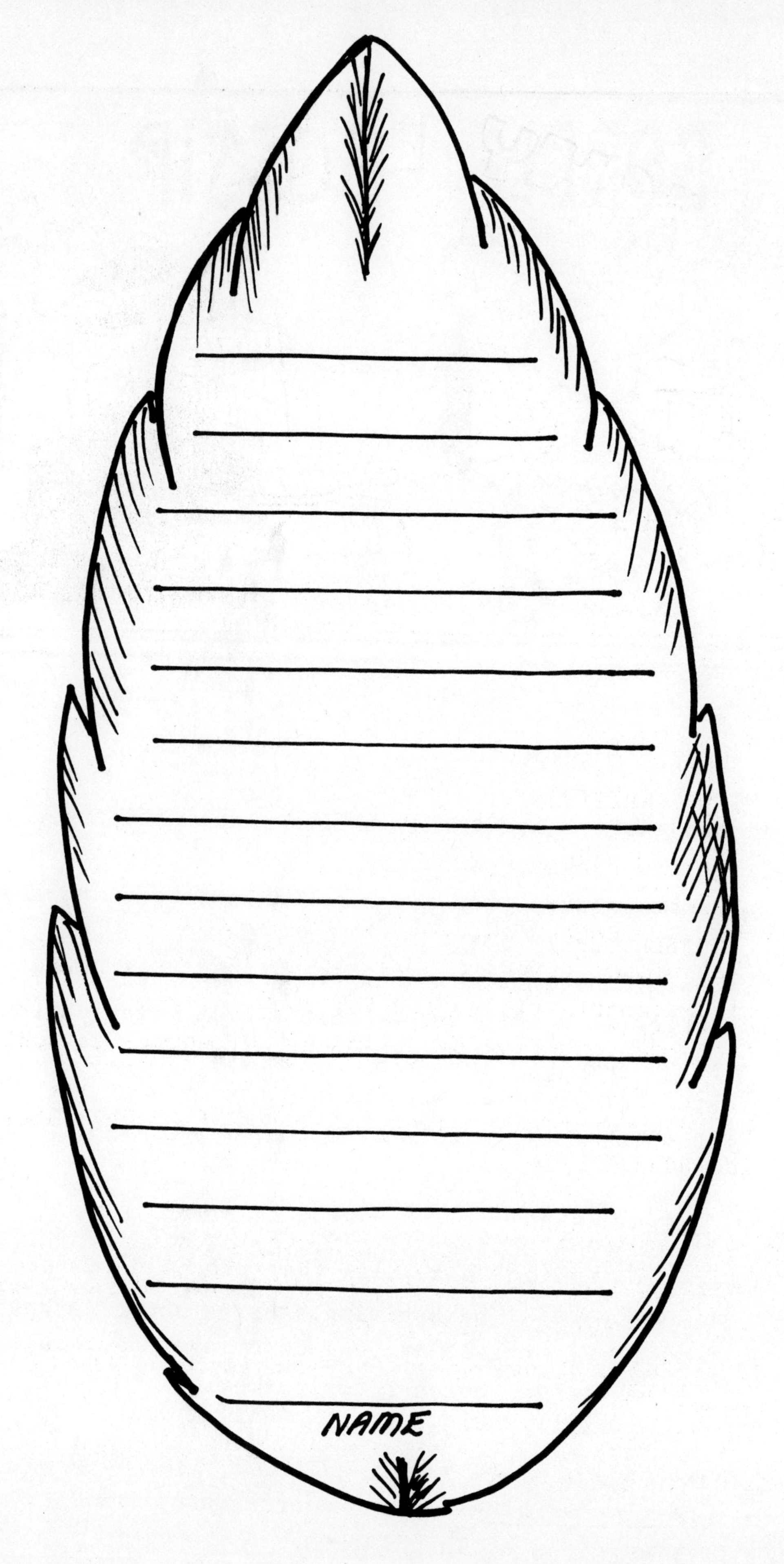
NAME

TITLE: WITCHY WRITINGS

MATERIALS:

1. Yellow background paper
2. A drawing or picture of a witch
3. Black construction paper for pot
4. Black construction paper for block letters to spell WITCHY WRITINGS
5. White construction paper for puffs of smoke (pattern included)

USE IN CONTENT AREAS:

1. Math-Use in helping student convert standard measurements to metric equivalents.
2. Spelling-List new words for studying on puffs of smoke.

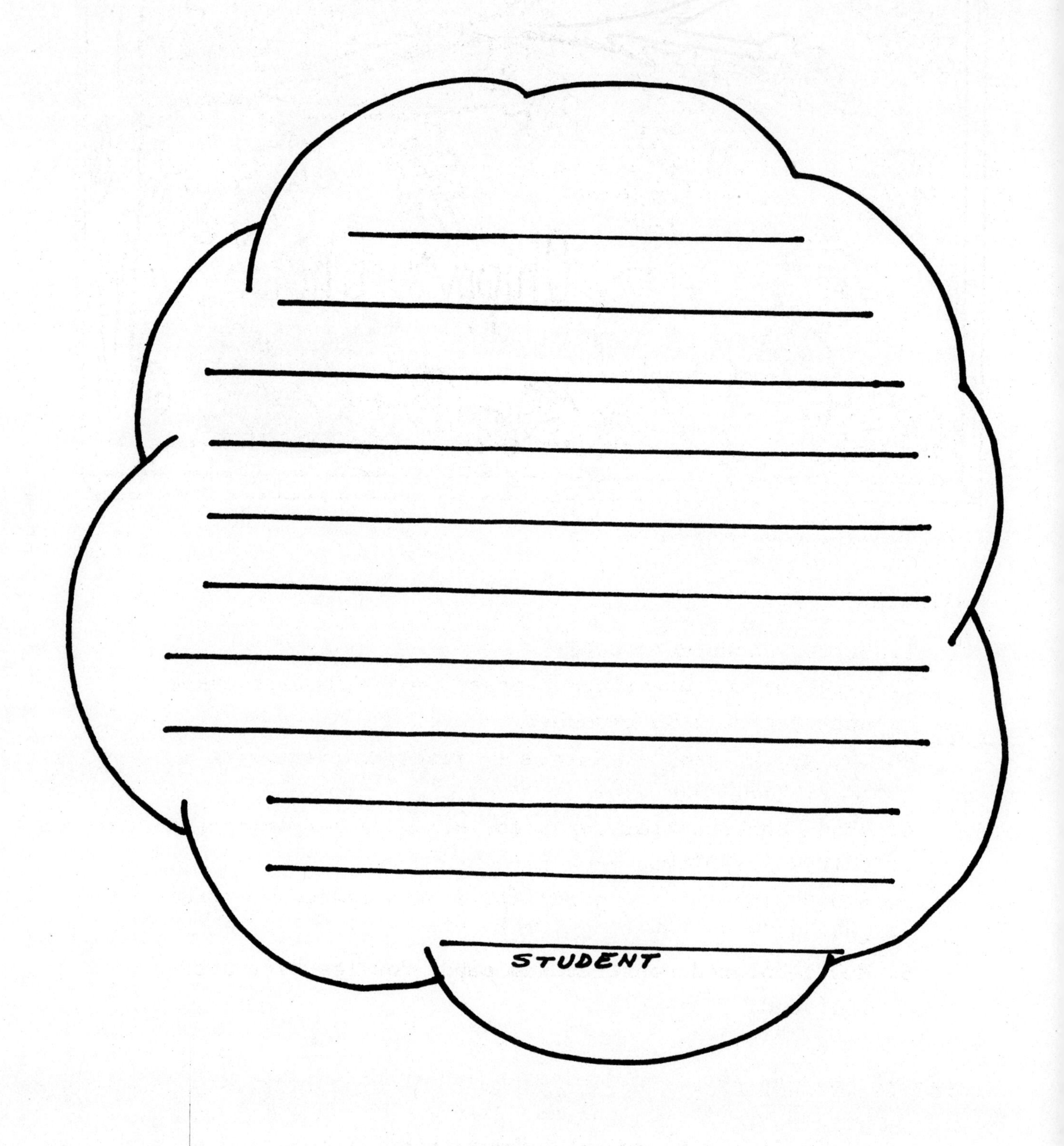
STUDENT

TITLE: CHIPPY'S CHOICES

MATERIALS:

1. Yellow background paper
2. Large brown construction paper tree with wide trunk and several long branches
3. Two large brown squirrels to place in tree or on stump under it
4. Brown construction paper for block letter to spell CHIPPY'S CHOICES
5. Brown construction paper for acorns (pattern included)
6. Multi-colored construction paper for leaves (pattern included)

USE IN CONTENT AREAS:

1. Science-Assign reports about trees, leaves and nuts.
2. Science-Following a study of the season, children can then write a story about autumn.
3. Math-Problems of any kind can be written on leaves and matched with answers on acorns.

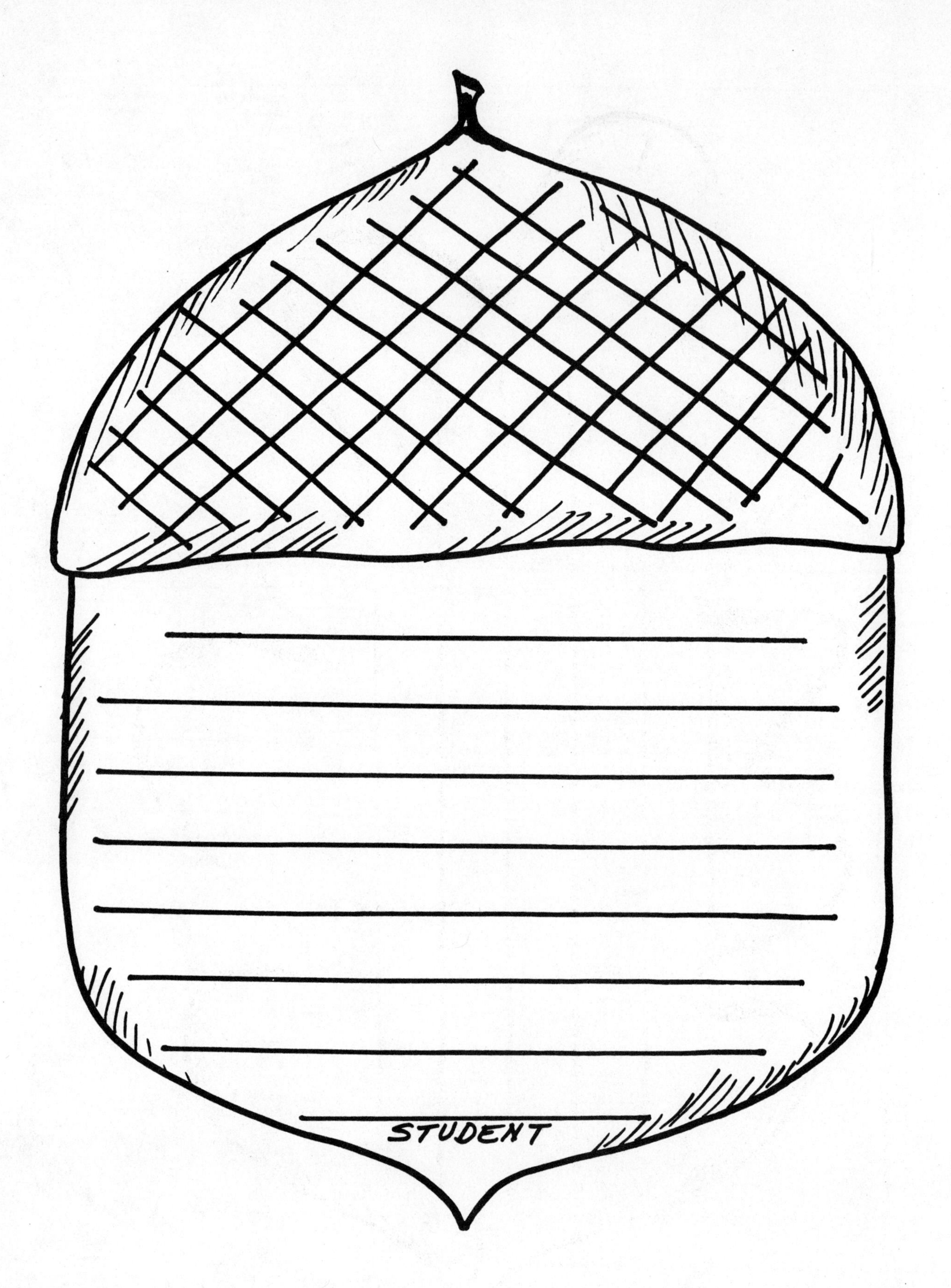
STUDENT

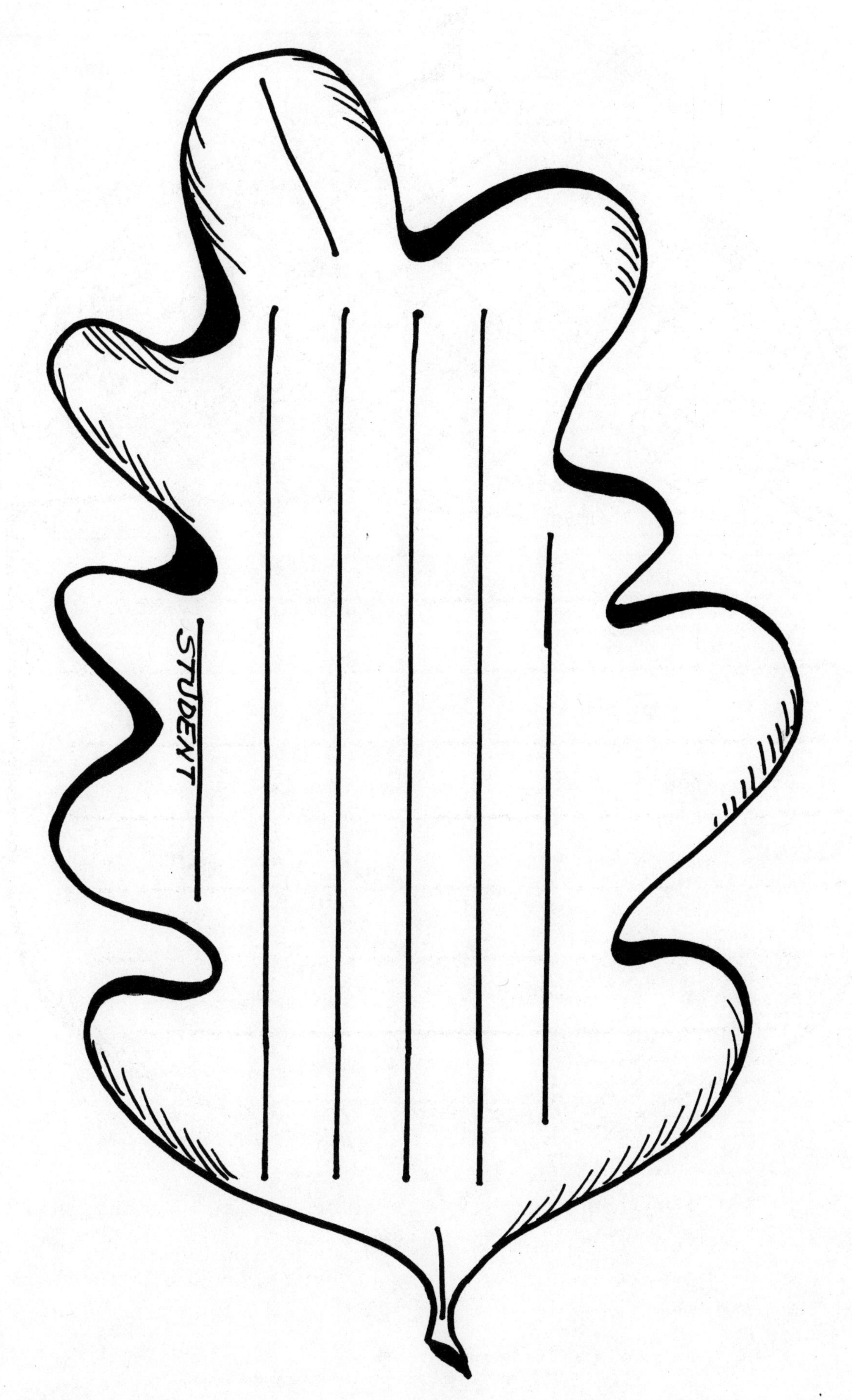
STUDENT

TITLE: TRIM THE TREE WITH GOOD WRITING

MATERIALS:

1. White background paper
2. Red paper for thin letters to spell
   TRIM THE TREE WITH GOOD WRITING
3. Large green Christmas tree branches made from green construction or wrapping paper
4. Yellow construction paper star or three-dimensional tree decoration for top
5. Various colors of construction paper for bells, candy canes, and tree ornaments (pattern included)
6. Small empty boxes (optional) to be wrapped and stapled under tree

USE IN CONTENT AREAS:

1. Math-Place various story problems or simple calculations on ornaments.
2. Social Studies-Assign reports about various countries and their customs on Christmas.
3. Spelling-Christmas vocabulary words can be placed on tree decoration.
4. Creative Writings-Pretend "You are a toy that fell out of Santa's sleigh" and write a story.

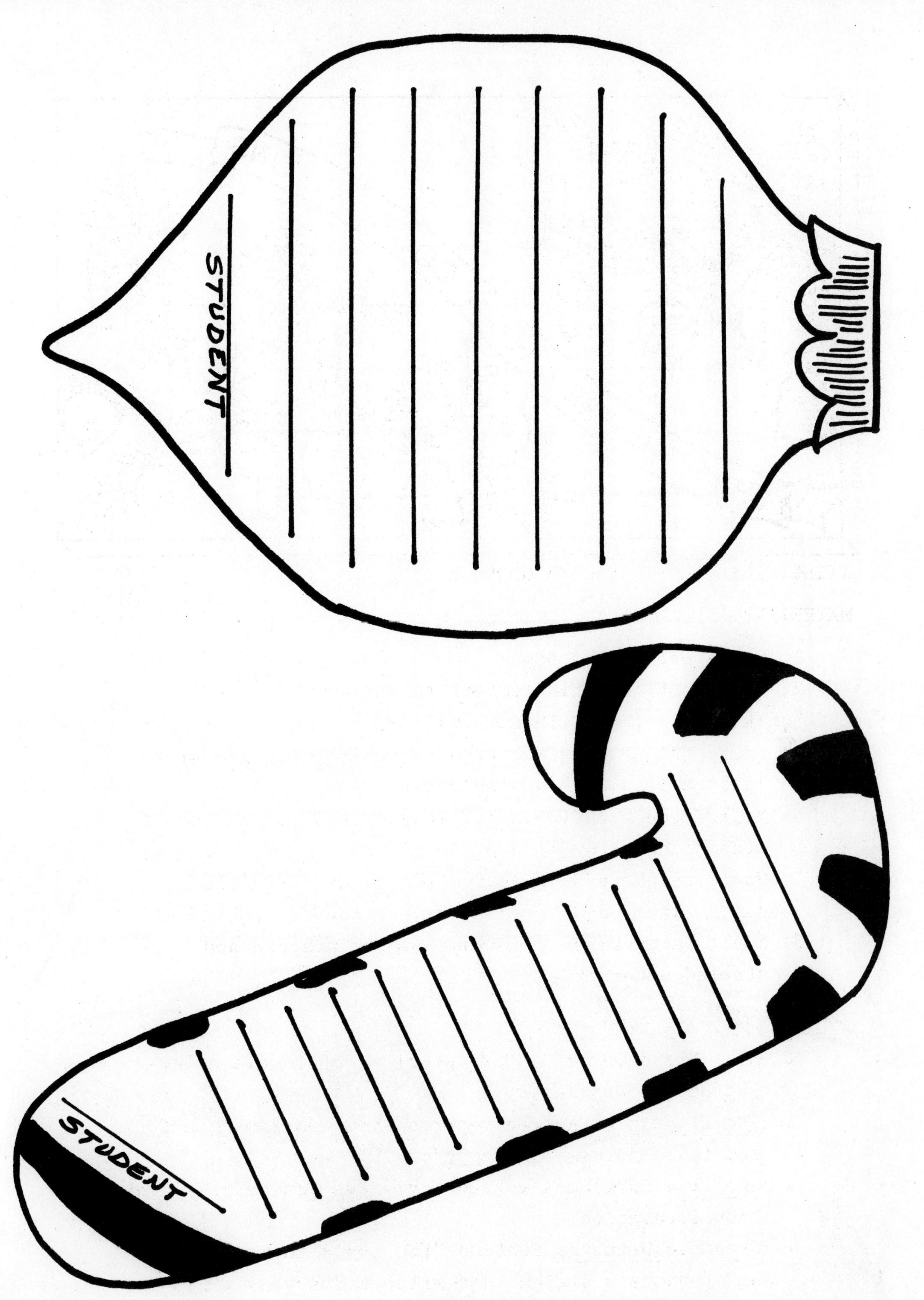
STUDENT
STUDENT

STUDENT

TITLE: LOVE GRAMS

MATERIALS:

1. Pink background paper
2. A red banner with large white block letters to spell LOVE GRAMS
3. White construction paper cut in the shape of a rectangle with the center cut out to resemble an envelope with a see-through front window
4. Red construction paper for hearts on which love notes/love grams are written and then placed behind the white paper envelope
5. Cellophane to cover window of white envelope (pattern included)

USE IN CONTENT AREAS:

1. Spelling-Place vocabulary words written on each heart in envelopes.
2. Social Studies-Write Valentine's Day customs on hearts.
3. Spelling-Use in rebus writing assignments.

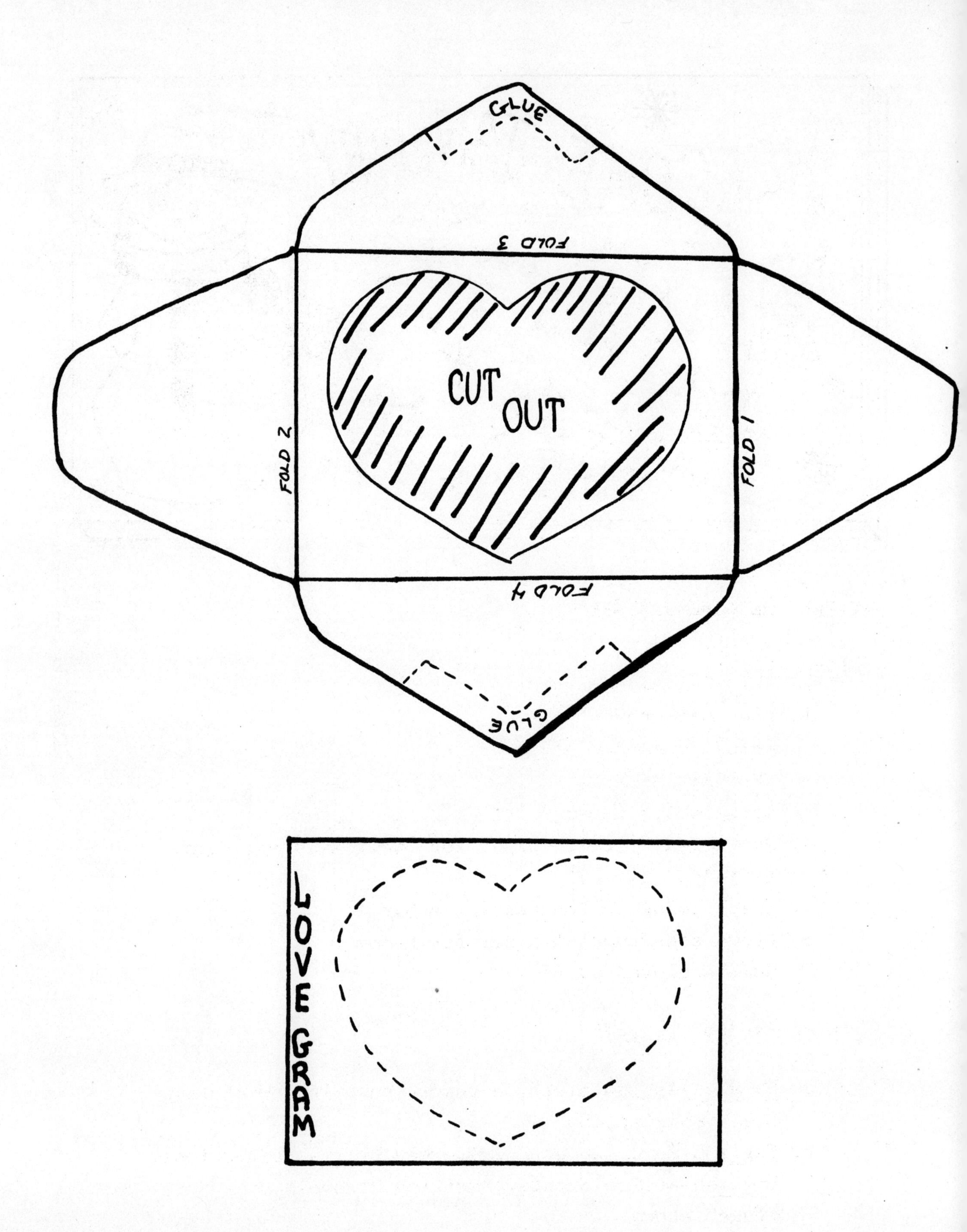
GLUE
FOLD 3
CUT
OUT
FOLD 2
FOLD 1
FOLD 4
GLUE
LOVE GRAM

TITLE: WELCOME JANUARY

MATERIALS:

1. Blue background paper
2. White construction paper for block letters to spell WELCOME JANUARY
3. Large white snowman
4. White construction paper for snowflakes (pattern included)
5. Black construction paper for hat
6. Brown construction paper for broom
7. Multi-colored scarf

USE IN CONTENT AREAS:

1. Science-Assign research report entitled "What is a Real Snowflake?"
2. English-Have students write New Year's resolutions.
3. English-Assign creative writing "Travels of a Snow-flake" story.
4. Music-Students write about their favorite winter song.

STUDENT

TITLE: A WREATH OF GOOD WRITING

MATERIALS:

1. White background paper
2. Red construction paper for holly berries and block lettering to spell A WREATH OF GOOD WRITING on leaves
3. Green construction paper for holly leaves to be outlined with black (pattern included)
4. Red construction paper or wide ribbon for large bow to be attached to bottom of wreath

USE IN CONTENT AREAS:

1. Science-Students write short reports about various winter plants or leaves.
2. Creative Writing-Assign stories about Christmas or winter.
3. English-Names of winter holidays can be studied with capital letters and apostrophes.
4. Math-Put problems of any kind on holly leaves with matching answers on berries.

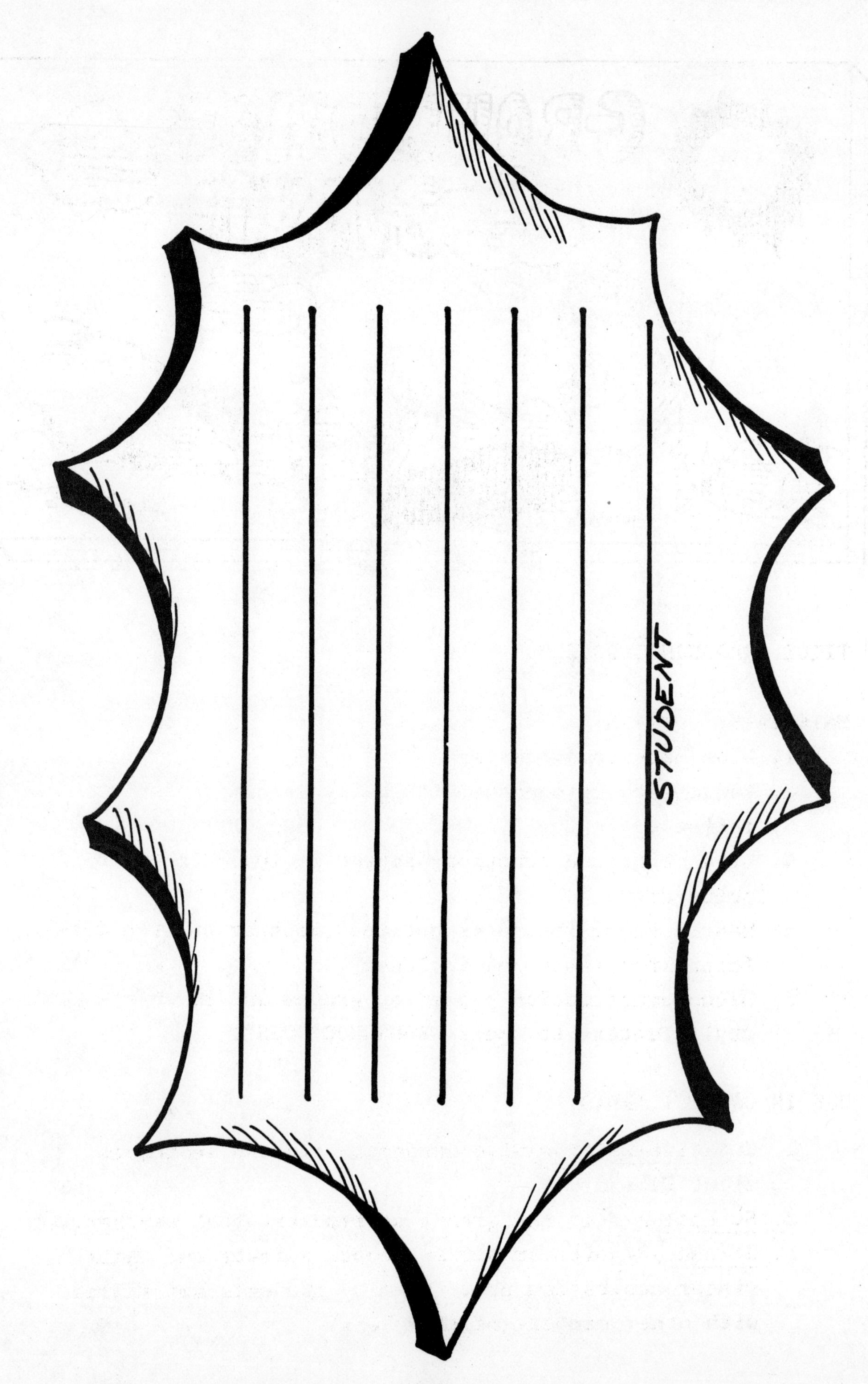
STUDENT

TITLE: GROUNDHOG GOSSIP

MATERIALS:

1. Blue background paper
2. Large brown groundhog with black shadow
3. Yellow sun
4. Light blue construction paper for clouds (pattern included)
5. Manila paper for rocks outlined with brown (two different rock patterns included)
6. Brown construction paper for ground and for block style letters to spell GROUNDHOG GOSSIP

USE IN CONTENT AREAS:

1. Creative Writing-Give students open-end sentences about February.
2. Science-Assign paragraphs or reports about weather.
3. Science-Reports or stories about animals and their winter habits can be written by students and shared with other members of the class.

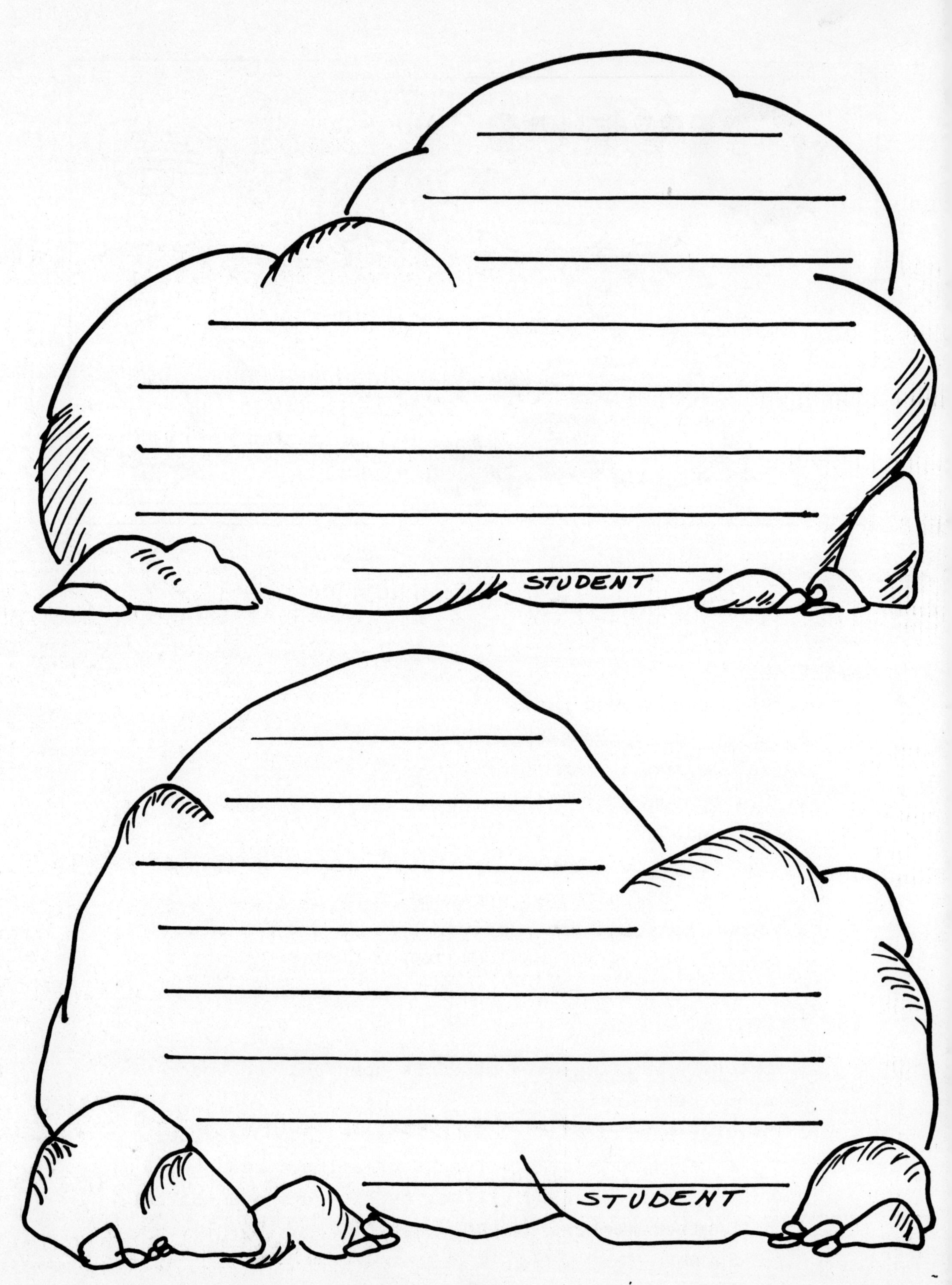
STUDENT
STUDENT

TITLE: WINTER'S WINNERS

MATERIALS:

1. Blue background paper
2. White construction paper for block letters to spell WINTER'S WINNERS
3. A colorful neck scarf
4. A black top hat
5. Eyes, nose, mouth and buttons cut out of black construction paper
6. White construction paper for snowballs (pattern included) to be positioned in the shape of a snowman

USE IN CONTENT AREAS:

1. Math-Place individual problems on snowballs.
2. Science-Individual reports of winter weather, clouds or temperatures could be written on the snowballs.
3. English-Assign creative writing lesson titled, "The Snowman That Wanted to Live in Florida but..."

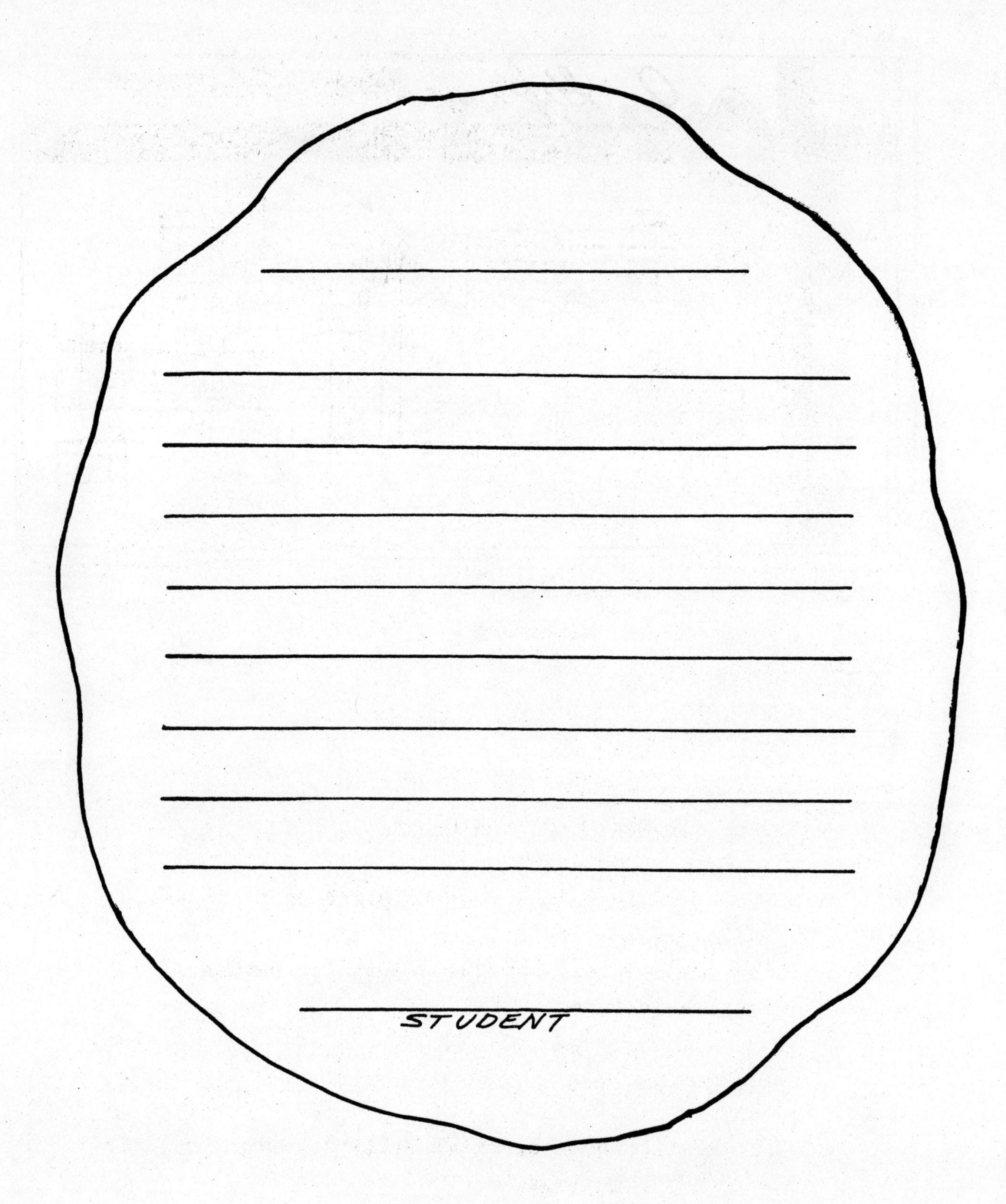
STUDENT

TITLE: A GIFT OF GOOD WRITING

MATERIALS:

1. Green foil paper background
2. Large red velvet bow
3. Red velvet ribbon
4. Black cursive lettering to spell
   A GIFT OF GOOD WRITING
5. Variety of Christmas bows to place on packages
   (optional)
6. Constuction paper-several colors for packages
   (pattern included)

USE IN CONTENT AREAS:

1. English-Develop a creative writing assignment using Christmas greetings.
2. Math-Develop story problems about toys and Santa's workshop.
3. Math-Catalog illustrations could be placed on packages. Children will then estimate prices of gifts and check with actual prices placed behind packages.

TO
NAME:

TITLE: OUR NEW YEAR'S RESOLUTIONS

MATERIALS:

1. Blue background paper
2. White construction paper for block letters to spell OUR NEW YEAR'S RESOLUTIONS
3. Two large white champagne glasses trimmed in black
4. Glitter placed on glasses to create effect of being full
5. New Year's party hats, streamers, noise-makers
6. White construction paper for bubbles (pattern included)

USE IN CONTENT AREAS:

1. English-Students write New Year's resolutions.
2. English-Assign creative writing task: "The Life of a Bubble."
3. Social Studies-Research New Year's celebrations in other lands.

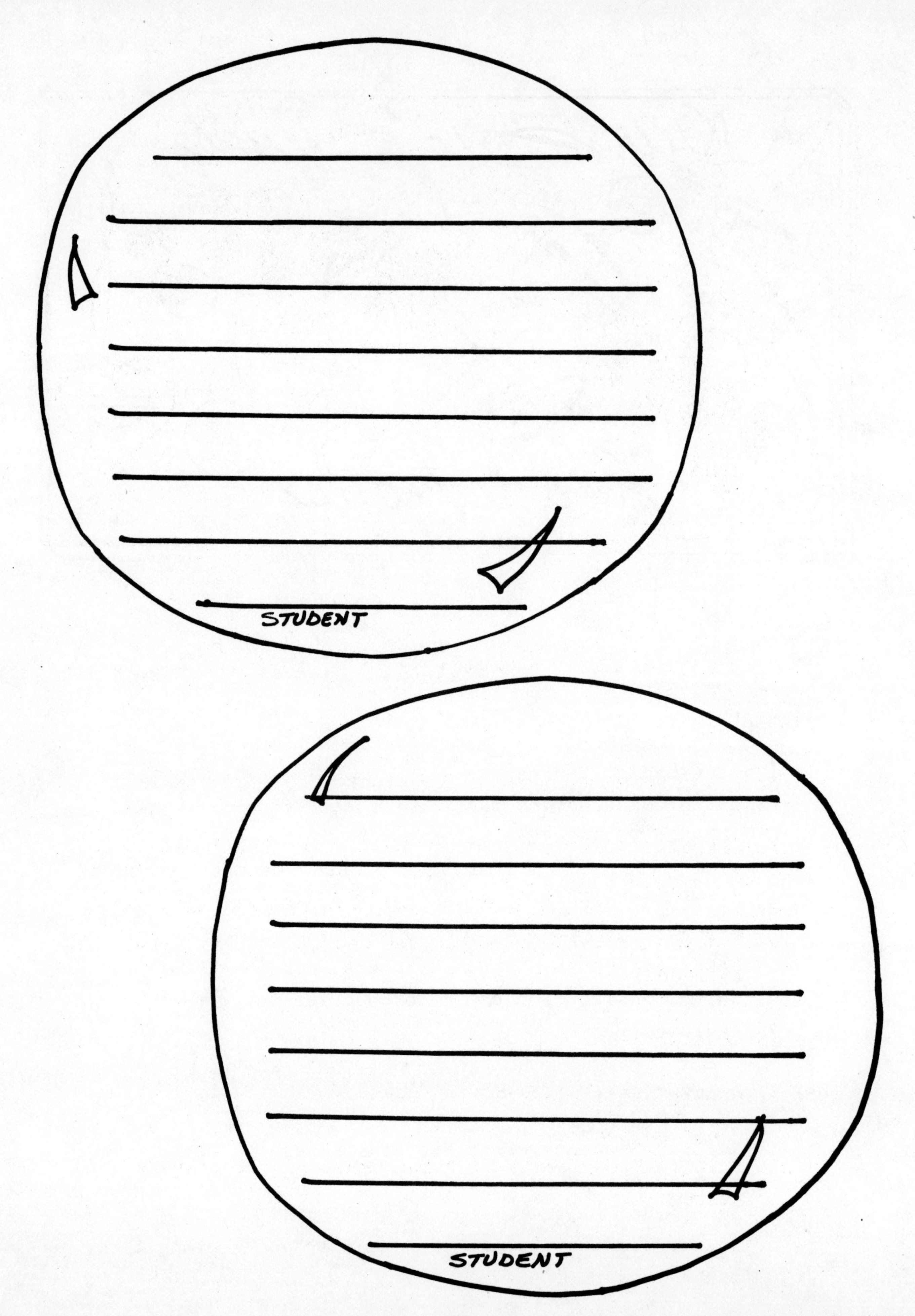
STUDENT
STUDENT

TITLE: LOVE NOTES

MATERIALS:

1. White background paper
2. Red construction paper for block letters to spell LOVE NOTES
3. White doilies on which the hearts can be placed
4. A large red lovebird
5. Red and white streamers interwoven between hearts
6. Red construction paper to cut hearts out (pattern included)

USE IN CONTENT AREAS:

1. Handwriting Lesson-Have students write a "special poem" on hearts.
2. Science-Study parts of human heart or circulatory system.

STUDENT

TITLE: SUPER POPS

MATERIALS:

1. White background paper
2. Red construction paper for block letters to spell SUPER POPS
3. Tongue depressors
4. Construction paper-several bright colors for lollipops (pattern included)
5. Plastic wrap-clear or colored

USE IN CONTENT AREAS:

1. English-Develop a creative writing assignment for Father's Day wishes.
2. Social Studies-Assign research on famous fathers (examples: Benjamin Franklin-Father of Invention; George Washington-Father of our country).
3. English-Students create Special Pop Awards: (examples: Handsome Hunter, Favorite Fisherman, and Goofy Golfer).

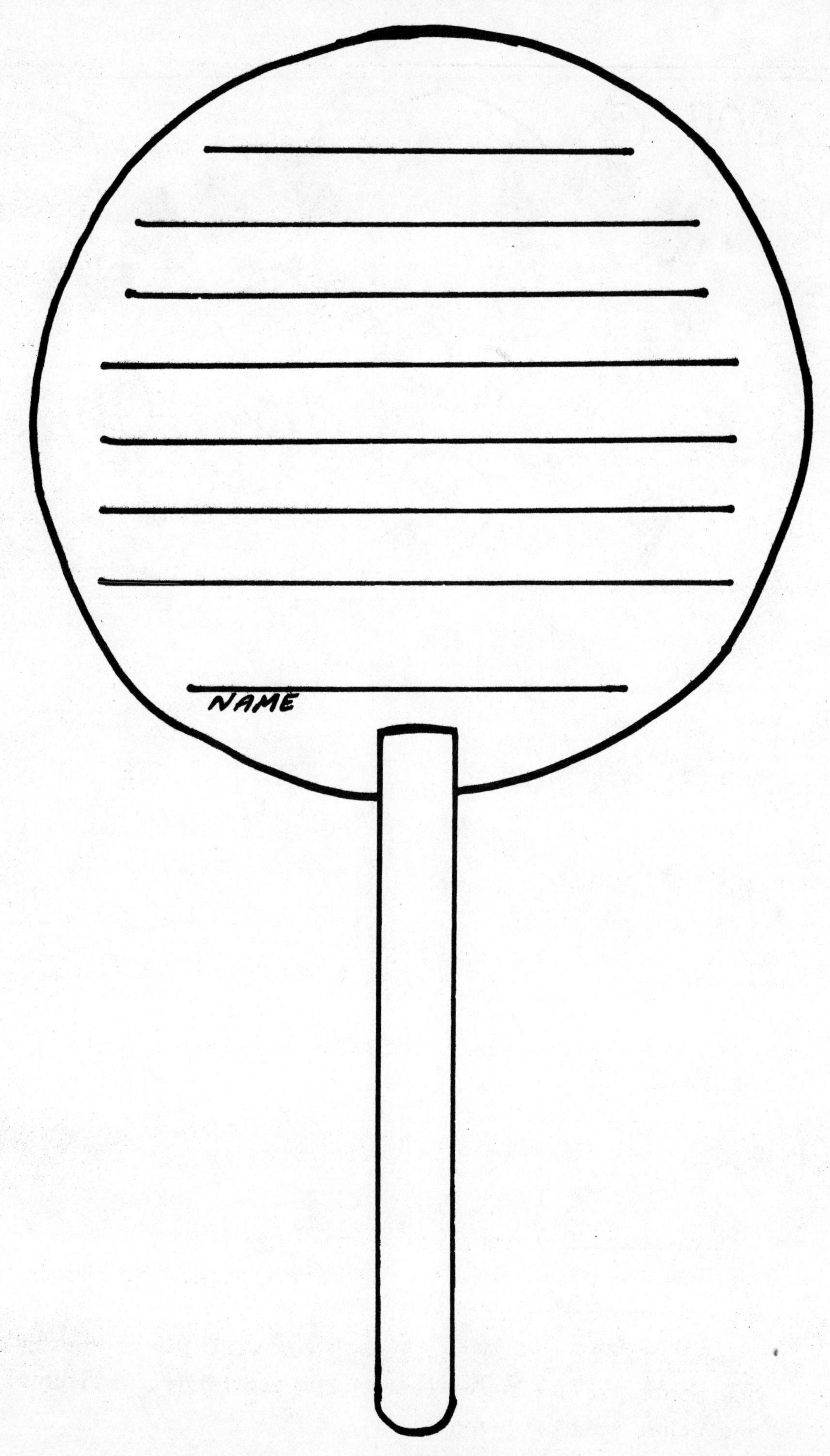
NAME

TITLE: CRACK OPEN A NEW MONTH

MATERIALS:

1. Dark blue background paper
2. Large white egg cracked into two pieces outlined with black marker
3. Yellow construction paper for ducks (pattern included)
4. Yellow construction paper for block letters outlined in black to spell CRACK OPEN A NEW MONTH
5. Green construction paper cut and fringed for grass under egg

USE IN CONTENT AREAS:

1. Science- Use with study of embryology.
2. Art-Have children draw the different stages of growth from an egg to a duck.
3. Calendar-List the activities that will occur during the month on the ducks (examples: birthdays, holidays and other special events).

STUDENT

TITLE: GRADE "A" EGGS

MATERIALS:

1. Yellow background
2. Large white Easter basket outlined with black
3. Construction paper-several bright colors for eggs (pattern included)
4. Purple construction paper for block letters to spell GRADE "A" EGGS
5. Green construction paper cut and fringed for grass under basket
6. Easter straw (any color) to be placed in basket around paper eggs to give 3-D effect
7. A ribbon or bow can be attached to basket for 3-D effect

USE IN CONTENT AREAS:

1. Science-Incubate eggs and have children write reports or facts on eggs.
2. Math-Individual story problems about Easter, eggs, chickens, candy or ducks could be written on eggs.
3. English-For use in creative story writing or in studying poems.

STUDENT
STUDENT

TITLE: SCHOOL'S OUT

MATERIALS:

1. Blue background paper
2. Green construction paper for seaweed
3. Black construction paper for letters to spell SCHOOL'S OUT
4. Assorted colors of construction paper for fish (pattern included)
5. Large picture of a deep-sea diver

USE IN CONTENT AREAS:

1. Science-Assign oceanography reports or study different species of fish.
2. Sports-List the responsibilities a fisherman has and the proper use of his equipment.
3. Water Safety-Write safety tips about swimming, scuba diving, boating and skiing.

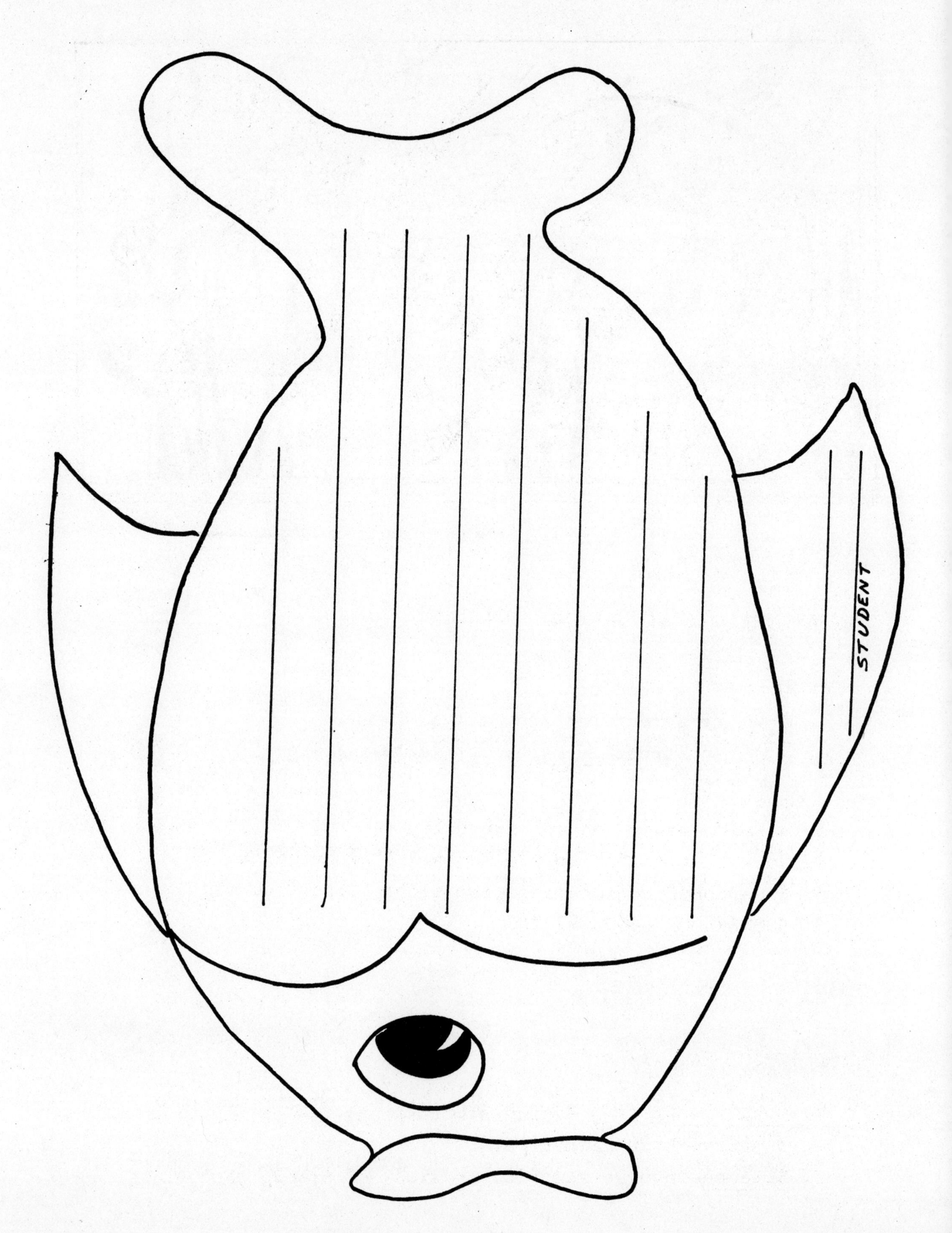
STUDENT

TITLE: SHOWERS OF GOOD WRITING

MATERIALS:

1. White background paper
2. Light blue construction paper for raindrops (pattern included)
3. A large multi-colored umbrella
4. Dark blue ribbon to tie on handle of umbrella
5. Blue construction paper for block letters to spell SHOWERS OF GOOD WRITING

USE IN CONTENT AREAS:

1. Creative Writing-Assign students the task of writing a story about raindrops.
2. Science-Involve students in study of precipitation.

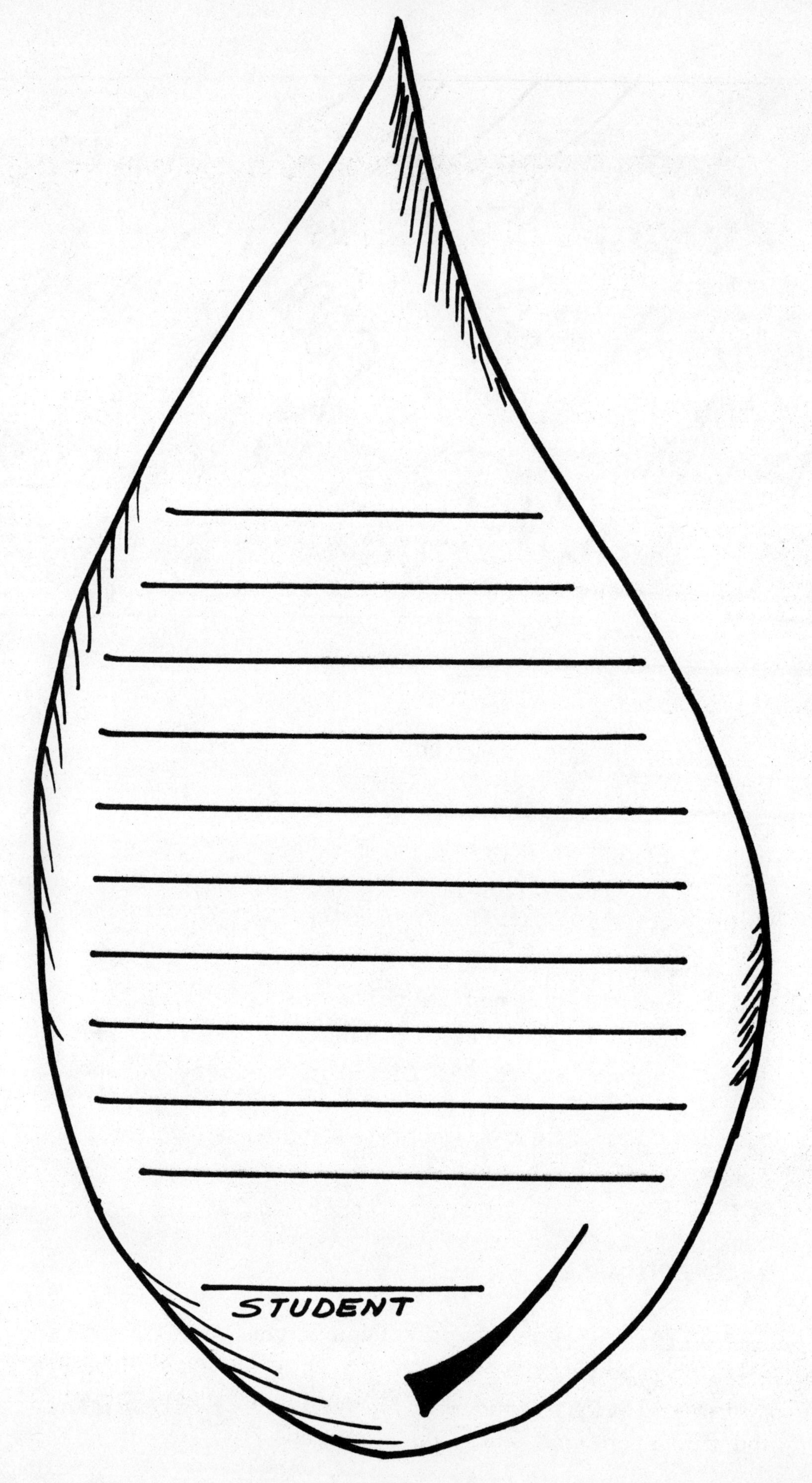
STUDENT

TITLE: PLANTING A NEW SEED-SON

MATERIALS:

1. White or yellow background paper
2. A large drawing of a farmer
3. Large green paper to form an awning above board
4. Black construction paper for block letters to spell PLANTING A NEW SEED-SON
5. Brown construction paper to make three baskets
6. Construction paper-several colors to make seed-like packages rectangular in shape (pattern included)
7. Draw a picture of different plants on package at top

USE IN CONTENT AREAS:

1. Science-Study plant life.
2. Math-Show multiplication facts on baskets and display problems to be worked on packages (addition, subtraction and division fact can also be used).

* CHILDREN DRAW IN SQUARE ANY FLOWER OR VEGETABLE OF THEIR CHOICE

TITLE: MOTHER, THE SWEETEST WORD I KNOW

MATERIALS:

1. Pink background paper
2. Black yarn or construction paper for a large musical staff plus lines and small, plain letters to spell MOTHER, THE SWEETEST WORD I KNOW
3. Green yarn or construction paper for vines around border
4. Green construction paper for leaves folded lengthwise to be placed along vines
5. Pastel or white construction or tissue paper for flowers to attach along vines
6. Black construction paper for notes cut slightly larger than white ovals to be glued over black notes (pattern for white oval notes included)

USE IN CONTENT AREAS:

1. English-Assign short poems about Mother to be written on each note.
2. Music-Put types of notes or various musical terms on each note.
3. Reading-Biographical sketches can be written about a child's mother.
4. Creative Writing-Have student relate funniest or fondest story about Mother.

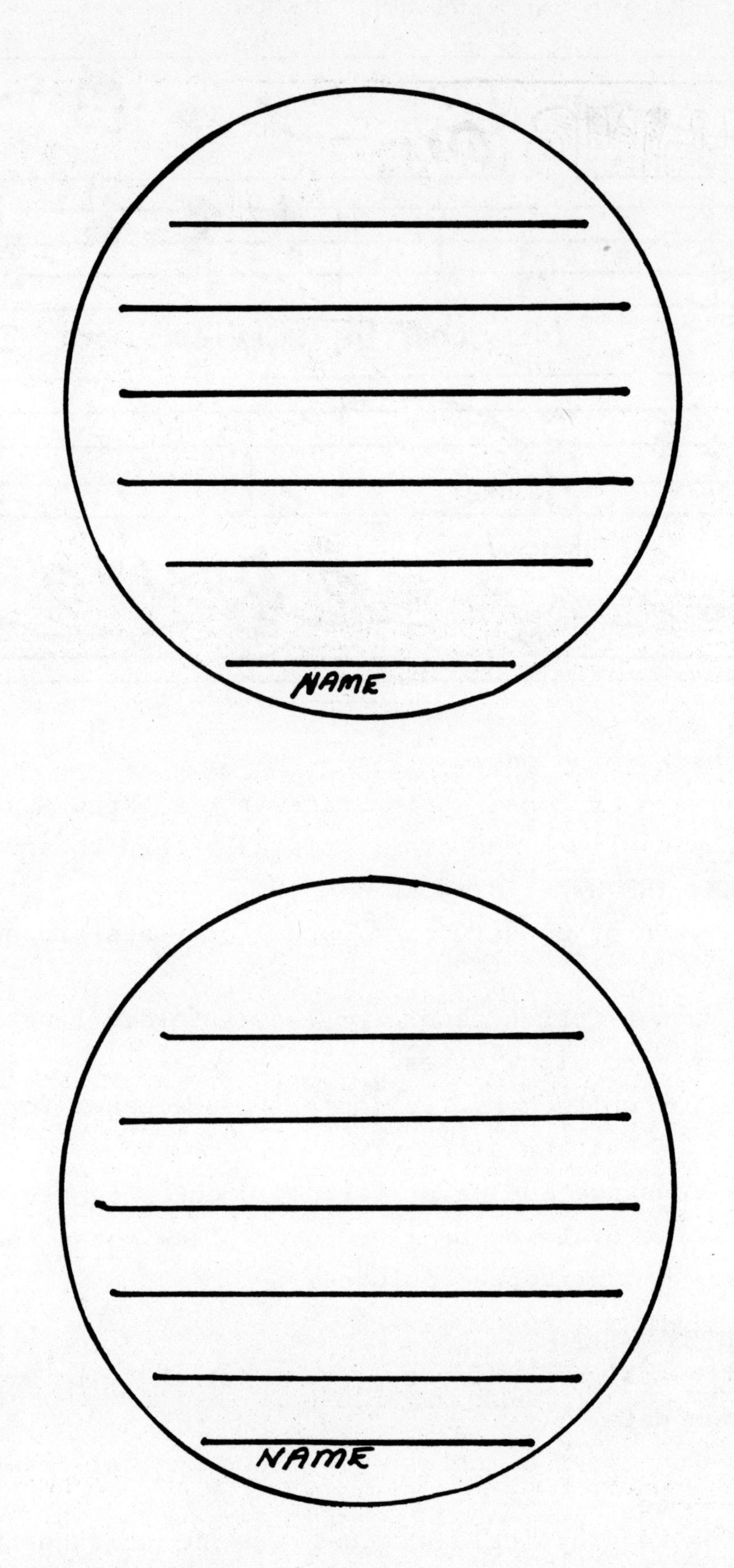
NAME
NAME

TITLE: SHELLING OUT FOR SUMMER

MATERIALS:

1. White background paper
2. Brown paper for beach
3. Dark blue paper for ocean
4. Enlarged drawing of conch shells and starfish
5. Green construction paper for block letters to spell SHELLING OUT FOR SUMMER
6. White shells outlined in black (pattern included)

USE IN CONTENT AREAS:

1. Science-Assign research projects on how sea shells are formed.
2. English-Have students write stories on "Summers at the Beach."
3. Math-Place individual math problems on shells.
4. Math-Create reading problems about the sea and place them on shells.

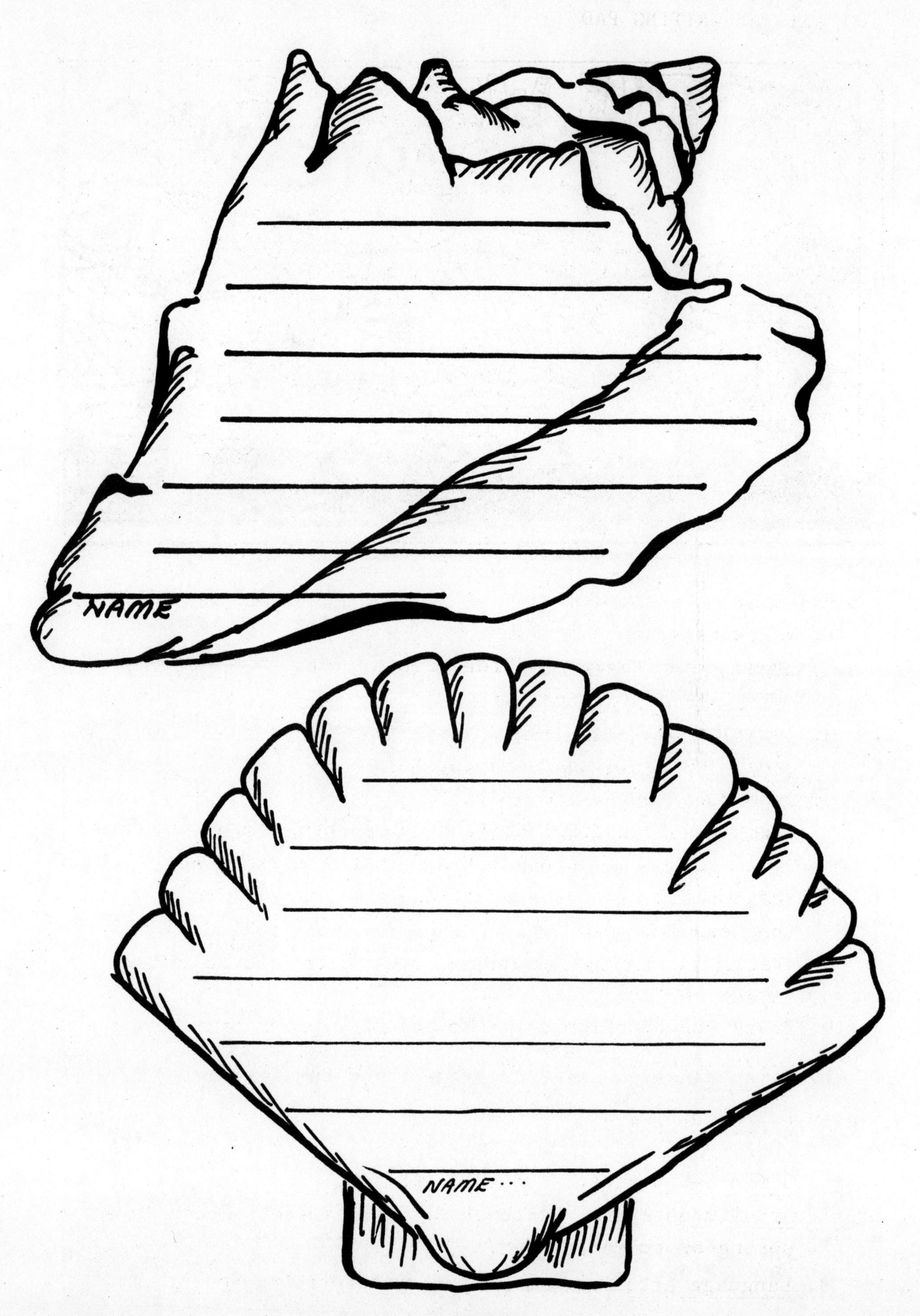
NAME
NAME...

TITLE: THE WRITING PAD

MATERIALS:

1. White background for sky
2. Light green background for hill
3. Dark blue background for water
4. Small brown mushrooms to place on hill
5. Green construction paper for lily pads
6. Dark blue letters to spell THE WRITING PAD with light green shadow letters to place behind blue letters
7. Green construction paper frogs (pattern included)
8. Red construction paper beetles with green heads (pattern included)
9. Yellow construction paper bees with orange wings (pattern included)
10. Black construction paper to accent various parts of frogs, beetles and bees

USE IN CONTENT AREAS:

1. Science-Study life cycle of the frog.
2. Art-Students draw sketches of other insects found in a spring or summer garden.
3. Language Arts-Read Haiku poetry describing Spring.

NAME

NAME

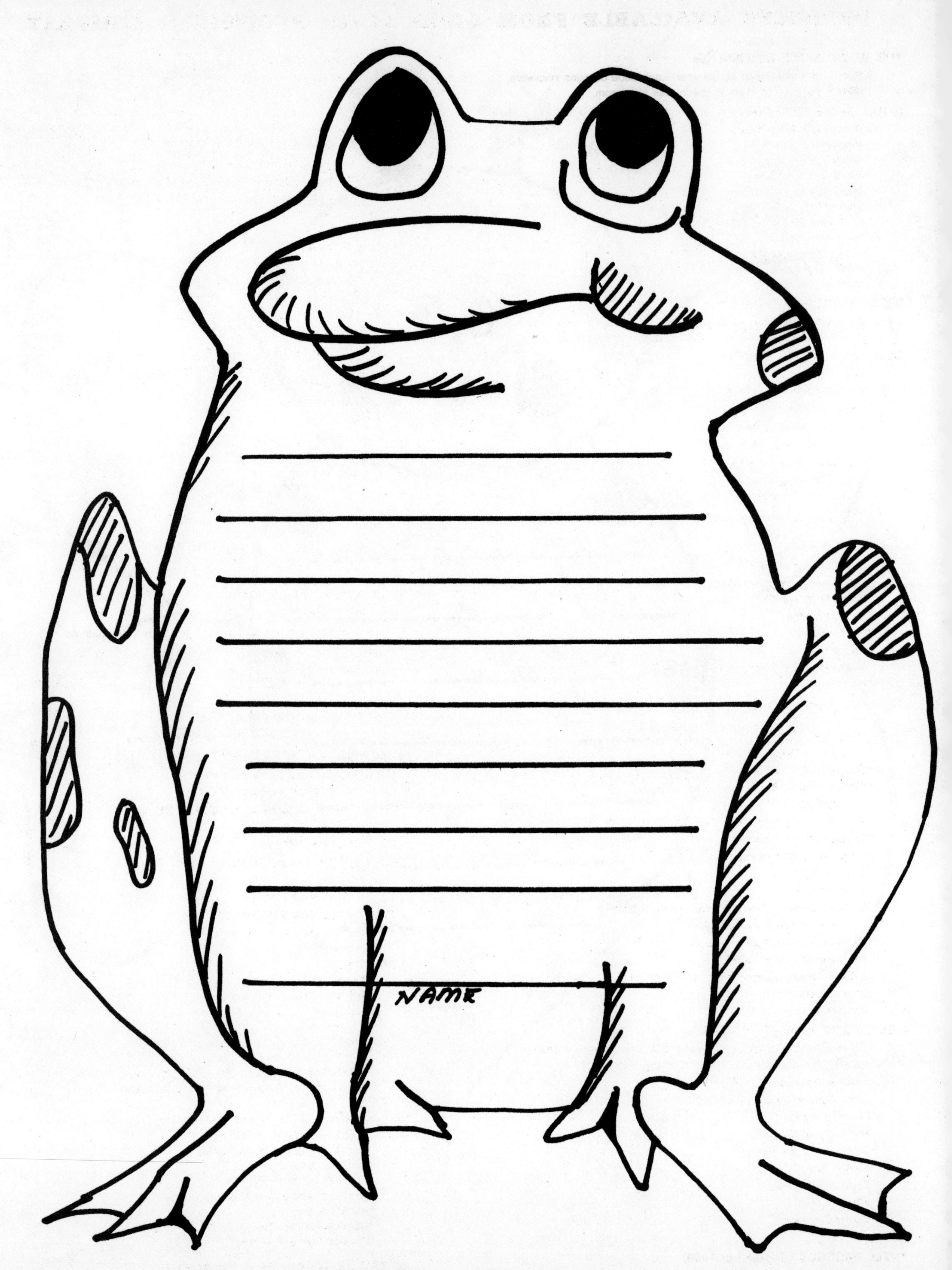
NAME